Animachines

by Debora Pearson
art by Nora Hilb

Annick Press
Toronto • New York • Vancouver

We acknowledge the support of the Canada Council for the Arts, the Ontario Arts Council, the Government of Ontario through the Ontario Book Publishers Tax Credit program and the Ontario Book Initiative, and the Government of Canada through the Book Publishing Industry Development Program (BPIDP) for our publishing activities.

The right of Debora Pearson to be identified as the Author of this Work has been asserted by her.

The publisher wishes to acknowledge with thanks Dr. Alison Preece, Associate Professor, Faculty of Education, University of Victoria.

Cataloging in Publication

Pearson, Debora
     Animachines / by Debora Pearson ; art by Nora Hilb.

ISBN 1-55037-797-3 (bound).—ISBN 1-55037-796-5 (pbk.)

     1. Animals—Juvenile literature. 2. Animal mechanics—Juvenile literature.
I. Hilb, Nora II. Title.

QL49.P42 2003   j591   C2003-900061-3

The art in this book was rendered in watercolor.
The text was typeset in Vag Rounded and Myriad Tilt.

Distributed in Canada by:
Firefly Books Ltd.
3680 Victoria Park Avenue
Willowdale, ON
M2H 3K1

Published in the U.S.A. by Annick Press (U.S.) Ltd.
Distributed in the U.S.A. by:
Firefly Books (U.S.) Inc.
P.O. Box 1338
Ellicott Station
Buffalo, NY 14205

Printed and bound in Canada by Friesens, Altona, Manitoba.

Visit us at: www.annickpress.com

For Liam Thomas Davison, always on the move
    —D.P.

To Marcela and Leandro
    —N.H.

stretch

A tall giraffe r-r-r-reaches up.
Hello, cherry picker truck!

fly

An albatross swoops and soars
up high. A jumbo jet thunders by.

race

A cheetah is a speedy runner.
Whoosh! A racing car really zooms.

dig

A badger and an
excavator claw and
scoop out holes.

dive

A whale drops down into the sea.
Sploosh! There goes a submarine.

pull

A pony tugs a wagon, clip-clop.
A tow truck hooks a car and chugs off.

crawl

A sea turtle creeps over the sand.

A bulldozer slowly treads by.

roar

A lion and a monster truck are loud.
Rumble, grumble, GR-R-R-R-ROWL!

squirt

An elephant gushes water.

A pumper truck spurts and sprays.

carry

An opossum lugs a cozy load.
A school bus vrooms by—who's inside?

goodbye